For Bella
— D. U.

For Barbara
— T. L. M.

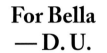

Henry Holt and Company, *Publishers since 1866*
Henry Holt® is a registered trademark of Macmillan Publishing Group, LLC
120 Broadway, New York, NY 10271 • mackids.com

ISBN 978-1-250-12709-9
Library of Congress Control Number 2019940941

Our books may be purchased in bulk for promotional, educational, or business use.
Please contact your local bookseller or the Macmillan Corporate and Premium Sales Department
at (800) 221-7945 ext. 5442 or by email at MacmillanSpecialMarkets@macmillan.com.

First edition, 2020 / Design by Sophie Erb
The illustrations for this book were created using Adobe Photoshop.
Printed in China by RR Donnelley Asia Printing Solutions Ltd.,
Dongguan City, Guangdong Province

10 9 8 7 6 5 4 3 2 1

DUCKS!

Deborah Underwood   illustrated by **T. L. McBeth**

GODWINBOOKS

HENRY HOLT AND COMPANY
New York

DUCKS!

NO DUCKS!

DUCKS?

NO DUCKS.

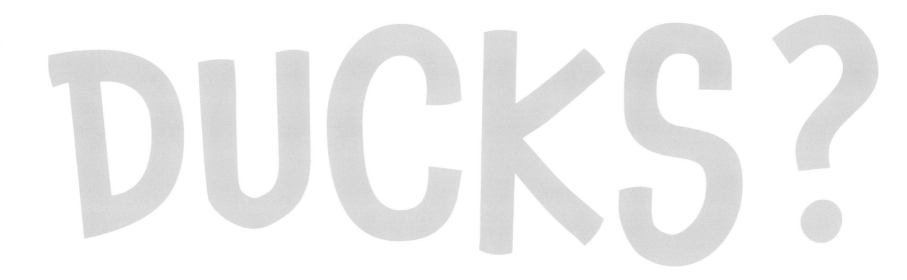

DUCKS?

NO DUCKS.

DUCKS?

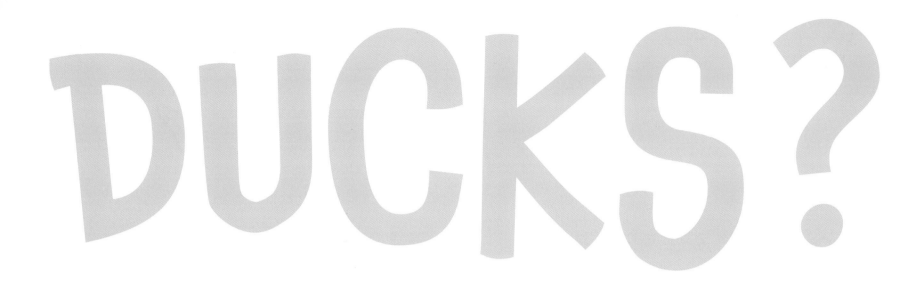

DUCKS?

NO DUCKS.

MOMMY?

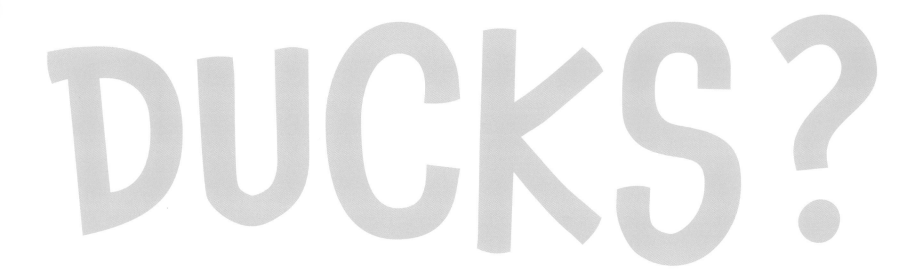

DUCKS?

DUCK
SALE